FOR AUBREY, SAWYER, ELLA, AND THE CHILDREN
TO COME —M.D. AND H.E.C.

FOR MOM, DAD, MICHAEL, AND CHARLEE—MAY THEY
ALWAYS HAVE HOPE BY THEIR SIDE. —C.L.W.

FOR GEM —H.C.B.

YOU ARE ALWAYS LOVED

A STORY OF HOPE

MADELEINE DEAN & HARRY CUNNANE

with CHELSEA LIN WALLACE

Illustrated by HOLLY CLIFTON-BROWN

RANDOM HOUSE 🏠 NEW YORK

Sometimes you look around,
and everything is bright and feels like love.

But if ever a storm blows through,
and you don't know how to feel,
know this—

When dark clouds cover the sun,
you are the light.

When the ground beneath you shakes,
and the winds swirl and push,
you are brave.

When you can't stop the lightning
or calm the crashing thunder,
you can look inside your heart,
where there's hope.

Hope is a friend helping you
soar above rough waters.

Hope is a friend carrying you up
mountains too hard to climb.

Hope is a friend who is
always by your side.

So, if ever a storm blows through

and something you cherish is swept away,

you are not the winds,

and you are not the rain,

and you are never alone.

And once the clouds have passed,
and everything around you is bright again,
know that you are always loved—

Rain or shine, all the time.

Dear Reader,

We wrote this book because we know all too well the effect of addiction on families.

I am Harry, and when my daughter was born, I was trapped in active addiction. I remember so clearly two things from the moment she came into the world: a fleeting hope that I would get better, and a lasting love for her that I knew would never wane. But addiction is powerful, and it was all-encompassing enough to keep me lost in turmoil for the first year of her life before I began active recovery. Through it all, I've wanted her to know one thing: that she is—and always has been—loved. Regardless of my addiction or recovery, my love was always there.

And I'm Madeleine—Harry's mom! I wanted to write this book to tell Harry how proud I am of him. I also wrote it as a mother who watched my son experience deep pain and, ultimately, lasting recovery. There were times in Harry's childhood when he was afraid. Don't we all feel that sometimes? Oh, how I wish I could have known more in those moments—helped him with his fear, made him understand that he could always lean on me and his father when he felt afraid or alone. That he was always loved.

We hope our book can be a place for children, parents, and caregivers to have conversations about difficult things and difficult emotions. For us, this story was inspired by our personal family journey. Whatever the struggle is in your family, it is possible to talk about it and to talk about how everyone gets scared—and that hope is in the love around us.

There are many wonderful resources available for families who need support. May our story be just one part of the boundless experience, strength, and hope that you find. And may it bring you the love and comfort that we have found in writing it.

With love,
Harry and Mad